For Rachel and Elena, and for their grandmother, B. J.
K. A.

For Felicia with thanks
T. T.

First edition 2003

Library of Congress Cataloging-in-Publication Data

Ayres, Katherine.
A long way / Katherine Ayres ; illustrated by Tricia Tusa.—1st ed.
p.   cm.
Summary: After a gift for her grandma arrives in the mail, a girl delivers
the present, transforming the box it came in into a variety of forms
of transport along the way.
ISBN 0-7636-1047-X
[1. Voyages and travels—Fiction. 2. Vehicles—Fiction.
3. Grandmothers—Fiction.] I. Tusa, Tricia, ill. II. Title.
PZ7.A9856 Lo 2003
[E]—dc21   00-039780

2 4 6 8 10 9 7 5 3 1

Printed in Italy

This book was typeset in Godlike.
The illustrations were done in ink, watercolor, and gouache
on Fabriano 140 lb. hot press paper.

Candlewick Press
2067 Massachusetts Avenue
Cambridge, Massachusetts 02140

visit us at www.candlewick.com

A Long Way

Katherine Ayres   illustrated by Tricia Tusa

CANDLEWICK PRESS
CAMBRIDGE, MASSACHUSETTS

Can I take this to
Grandma's house now?

It's a *long* way, but I
know how to get there.

First . . .

car

then . . .

boat

then . . .

airplane

then . . .

subway

finally . . .

feet   feet

feet.

Hooray!